"As Long as Grass Should Grow and Water Flow"

Argentina Palacios

Contents

Rigby

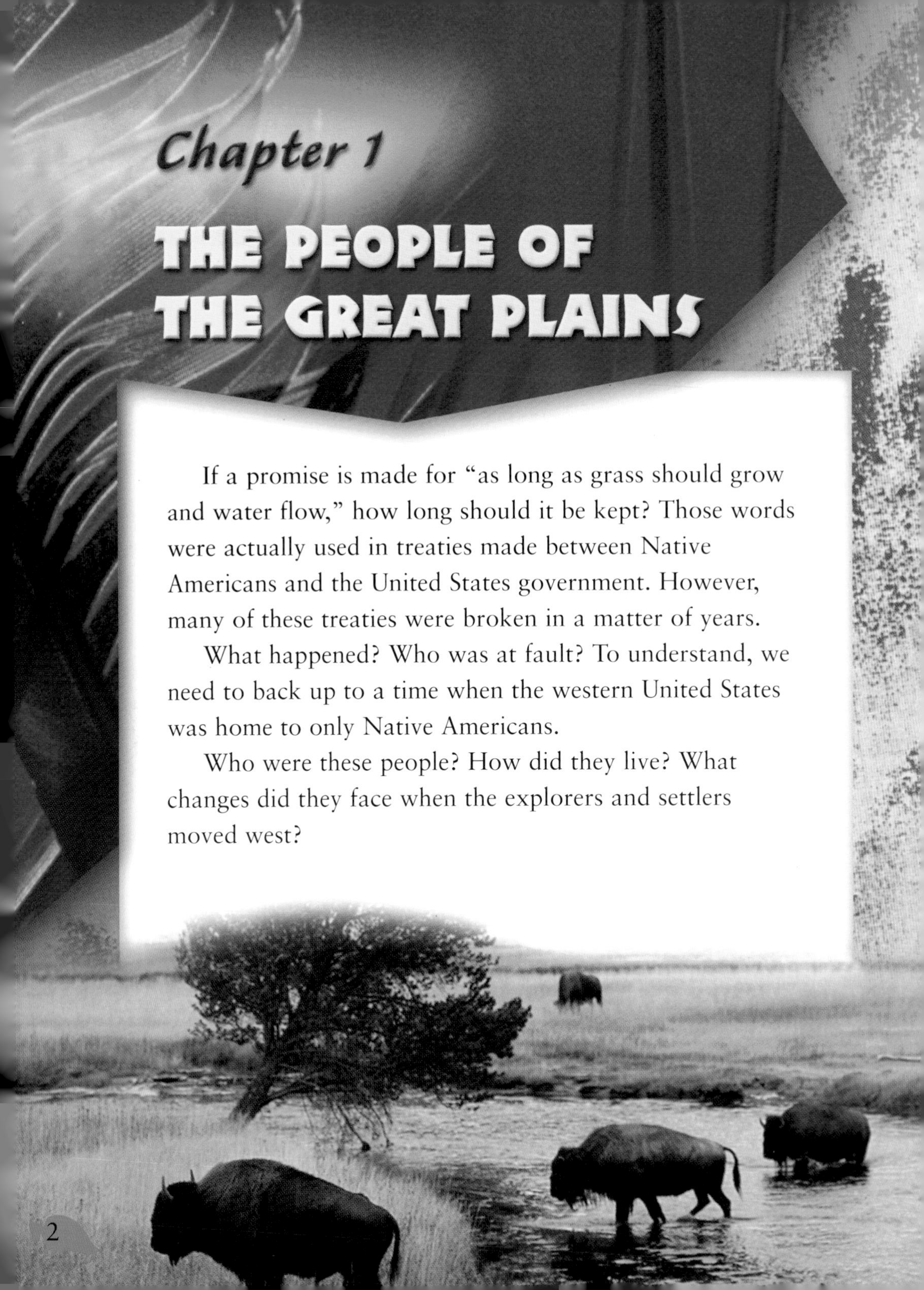

Chapter 1
THE PEOPLE OF THE GREAT PLAINS

If a promise is made for "as long as grass should grow and water flow," how long should it be kept? Those words were actually used in treaties made between Native Americans and the United States government. However, many of these treaties were broken in a matter of years.

What happened? Who was at fault? To understand, we need to back up to a time when the western United States was home to only Native Americans.

Who were these people? How did they live? What changes did they face when the explorers and settlers moved west?

The Seven Council Fires

In the middle of the nineteenth century, American and European settlers began moving west in great numbers. They found themselves in a territory that was already occupied. The Sioux was one group who lived on the Great Plains—a grassy area that included much of the middle of the continent.

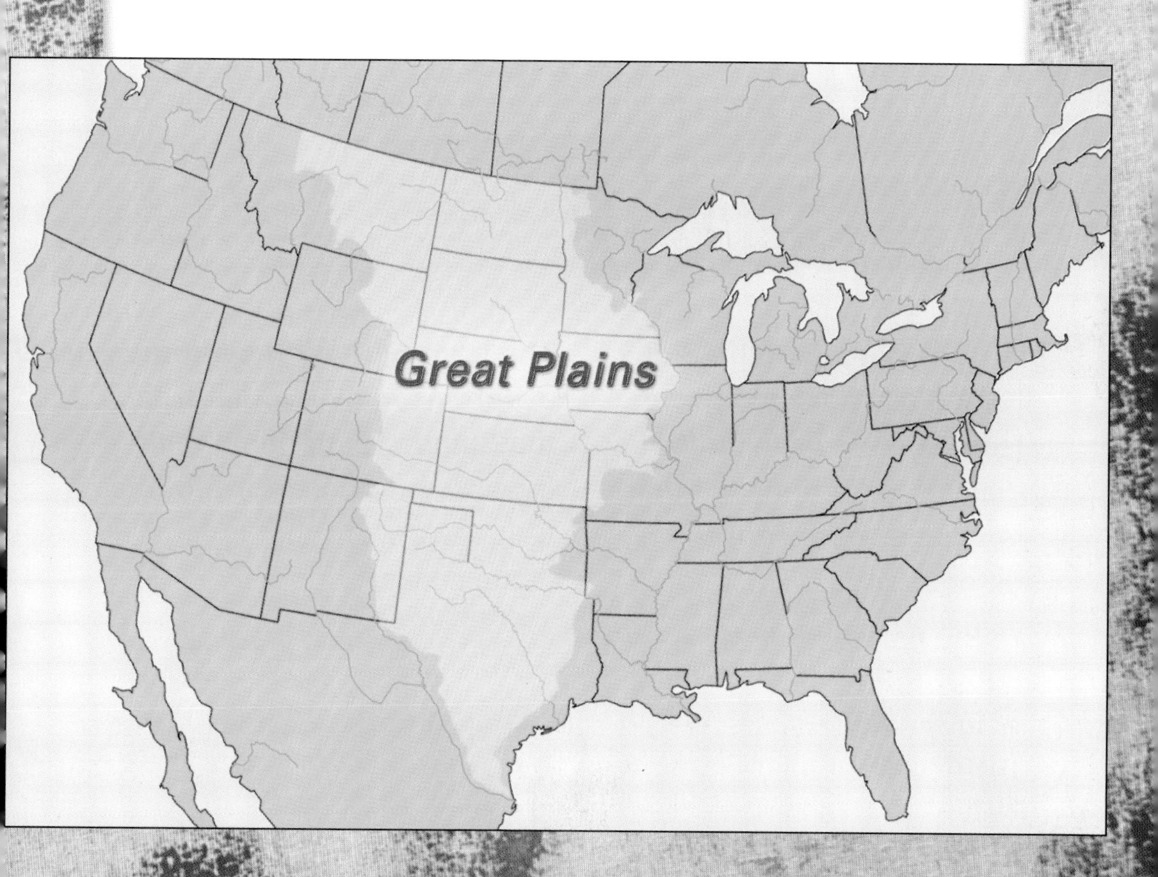

The Sioux Nation was actually made up of several groups with similar customs, habits, and beliefs. Together they formed what they called the Seven Council Fires.

These large groups were divided into much smaller units, each with its own council fire. At every level there were leaders, or chiefs. The chiefs had to be wise and brave, for they were expected to lead by example. They had no control over the daily activities of the people, but their influence was still enormous. The chiefs were the ones who decided to wage war or to make peace. Their decisions were followed by their people.

The people of the Sioux Nation all spoke the same language. However, different dialects, or varieties of that language, were spoken in different areas. The people actually referred to themselves by the names of these dialects—as the Lakota, Dakota, and Nakota.

The term *Sioux* comes from a word used by another tribe, the Chippewa, to name them. It was a shortened form of the Chippewa word that means "little snake."

Great Plains Migration

The Sioux had not always lived on the Great Plains. At one time, they lived near the source of the Mississippi River, in what is now Minnesota. Their diet consisted mainly of wild rice, fish, and game animals such as deer. They made their houses from wooden poles, earth, and bark. The Sioux traveled the many rivers of the area in canoes.

The Chippewa lived to the east of the Sioux. The two tribes fought constantly over territory, with the Sioux almost always losing. The Chippewa had two advantages. First, they outnumbered the Sioux. Second, they had better weapons—guns they had received in trade with the whites.

To escape the fighting, the Sioux began migrating west. They moved toward the Missouri River, where they found wide open prairies and herds of buffalo that numbered in the millions. By 1775, the majority of the Sioux lived on the Great Plains.

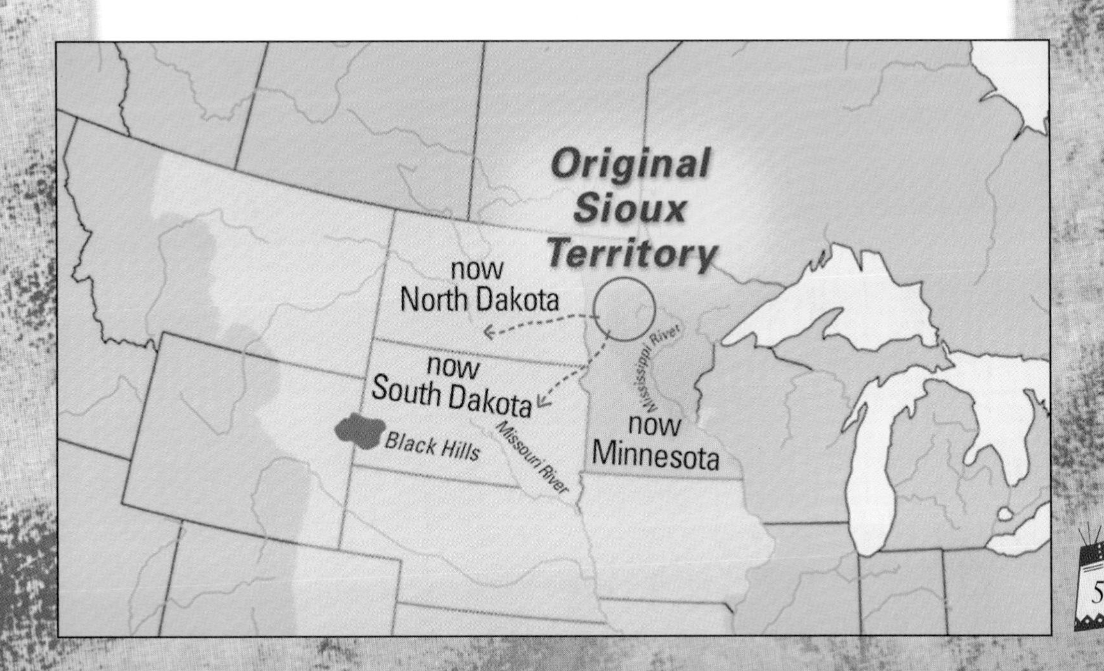

Following the Buffalo

A new home led to a new lifestyle for the Sioux. In the forests of Minnesota, they had lived settled lives, staying in one place. Now they became nomads, following the buffalo. Their homes were cone-shaped structures of wooden poles covered with animal skins. These homes, called tepees, were light and portable, and were perfect for a people who followed the herds. They could be set up and taken down in a matter of minutes.

The Sioux diet changed as well. Instead of rice, fish, and game, the people survived almost entirely on buffalo meat and wild berries.

A member of the Sioux stands in front of his tepee in this photo taken in 1891.

Two other important changes took place as well. First, the Sioux began to own horses. These animals were not native to America. They were brought to the continent by Spanish explorers of the Southwest. Tribes from that area then introduced horses to the tribes of the Great Plains.

Second, the Sioux began trading with French explorers, receiving guns in exchange for furs.

Now mounted on horseback and armed with guns, the Sioux became great warriors, ready to defend their territory.

Chapter 2

THE SIOUX WAY OF LIFE

In Sioux society, the roles of women and men were very different. Women were in charge of the household. They gathered berries, sewed clothing, and set up and took down the tepees. They skinned the buffalo and prepared its meat.

Men were the hunters and supplied their people with food. They were the warriors who defended their nation from enemies. Men had to prove themselves on the hunting grounds and in battle before they were allowed to wear the long, traditional feathered headdress.

A Sioux mother and child, early 1900s

Property and Wealth

The Sioux did not really understand the white man's ideas about owning property. To them, wealth was measured in horses. The more horses a person had, the richer he was. Trading horses was important. So was breeding, or raising, them. The Sioux preferred small horses because they were fast and sure-footed. So they tried to breed animals with these qualities.

The Buffalo Hunt

Sioux men usually went buffalo hunting twice a year. The main purpose of the hunt was to find food. After a successful kill, the people feasted for days on fresh buffalo meat. Some of the meat was dried so it would last for months. No part of the animal was wasted—the horns and bones became tools, utensils, and weapons. The thicker furs of buffalo killed in the fall were made into splendid robes, warm bed coverings, lodge floors, and linings. The lighter hides of summer buffalo were used for things like tepees and saddlebags. Buffalo hides were used to make clothing, moccasins, and war shields.

When the work was done, one large hide was given back to "Mother Earth." It was beautifully painted and left in a spot overlooking the hunting grounds.

Chapter 3
THE WHITE MEN COME

For a long time, the only white people the natives of the West came into contact with were explorers and traders. Then, in 1803, the United States became a much larger nation. The government purchased a large territory from France. This land, known as the Louisiana Purchase, stretched west from the Mississippi River to the Rocky Mountains. It extended north to the Canadian border and south to Mexico.

This painting shows the ceremony of land transfer for the Louisiana Purchase.

Louisiana
Purchase

In 1804, President Thomas Jefferson sent Meriwether Lewis and William Clark on a mission of exploration. On their journeys, Lewis and Clark and their fellow explorers came into contact with about 50 native tribes. They explained to each tribal chief that the lands they lived on now belonged to the United States. They told them that the Great Father—the chief of all chiefs—lived in the East. This news did not please the natives, especially the Sioux. They would not accept the idea that any one person or group of people could "own" the land. To them, it belonged to everyone.

Trading Posts and Trails

By 1834, the Sioux and other tribes were actively trading with white people. The Native Americans exchanged buffalo hides and fur from animals such as beaver and otter for goods they could not get by hunting, such as woven cloth. Some tribes even moved closer to the trading posts to make trading easier.

For years now, small numbers of adventurous men and women had been heading west. Then, in 1849, gold was discovered in California and huge numbers of people began

This illustration shows the settlers and Native Americans trading goods.

to migrate west. And that was only the beginning. Gold was discovered in areas other than California.

Soon wagon trains with hundreds of wagons were carrying entire families west. The most well-traveled trails became known by names like the California Trail and the Oregon Trail. These wagon trails passed through territory inhabited only by Native Americans.

The First Treaties

For the most part, the whites who were headed west wanted only to pass through the grassy Great Plains. They had no interest in settling there. They were looking for the treasures that lay further west in places like California and the Oregon Territory.

Even so, many of the Native Americans did not like what was happening. They attacked the wagon trains and raided camps whenever possible.

The United States government wanted to do something to protect westward travelers. So, in 1851, at Fort Laramie (in what is now Montana), several treaties were signed. In these treaties, tribal chiefs considered friendly to the whites agreed to allow wagon trains to pass peacefully through their lands. In exchange, the tribes received cash payments. These treaties also drew up boundaries between the territories of different tribes.

A few of the Native Americans who signed the treaties were minor chiefs of the Sioux Nation. However, most of the Sioux were angry at the thought of treaties with the whites. So were their allies, the Cheyenne and the Arapaho.

The Red Cloud War

In the 1860s, things began to change. The Great Plains started to become a destination for settlers. In 1861, the United States Congress officially created the Territory of Dakota. This area included what is now South Dakota, North Dakota, Montana, and most of Wyoming. The Homestead Act of 1862 allowed "non-Indians" to buy public lands cheaply.

Then, in 1863, the Union Pacific and Central Pacific railroad companies began working on a transcontinental

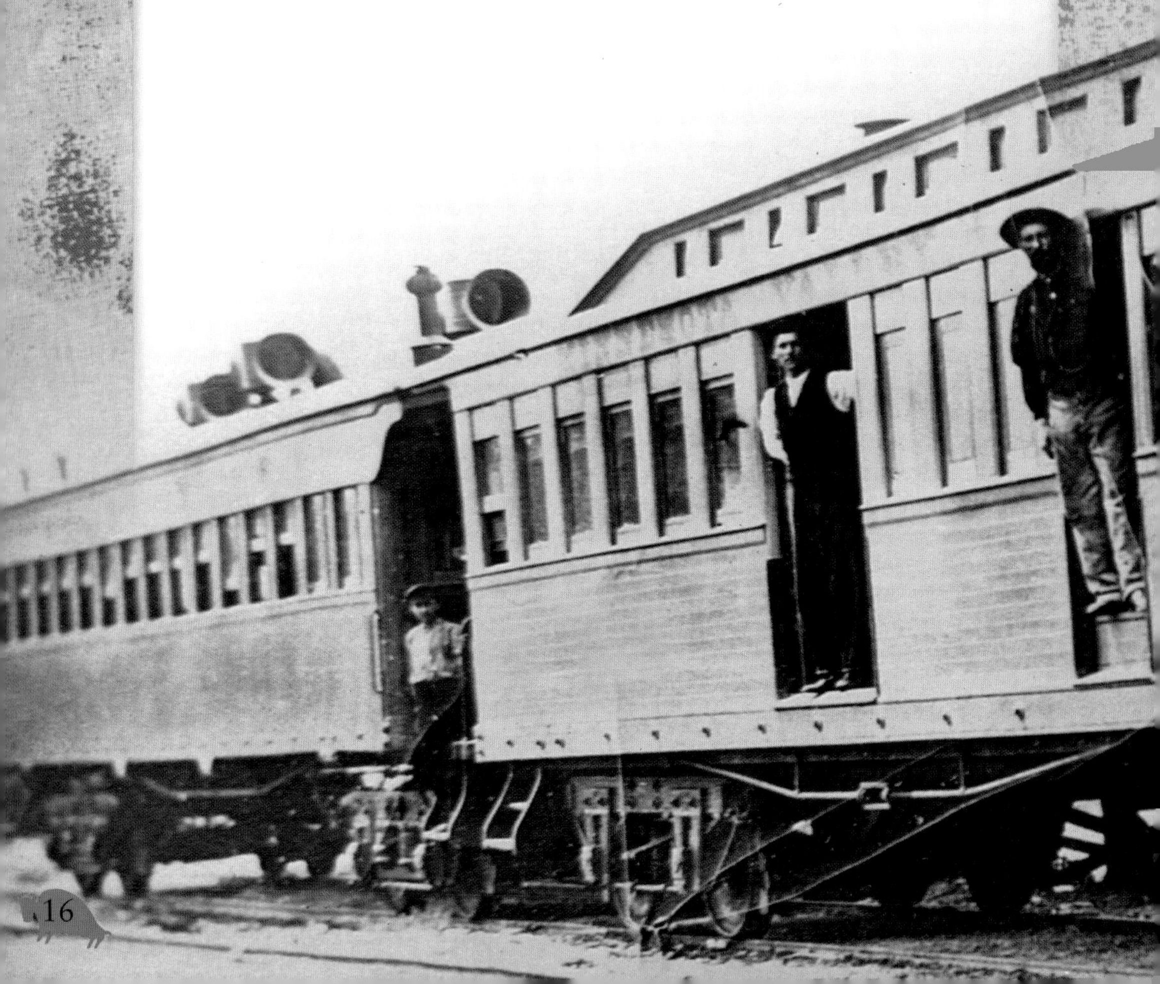

railroad. This would connect railroads across the country, making travel from east to west much easier. Work on the railroad took several years and was completed in 1869. The train tracks ran through the Great Plains.

Another event in 1863 made things even worse. A man named John Bozeman took a shortcut to the gold fields in Montana. The Bozeman Trail, as this new route was known, cut through the heart of Sioux territory. All-out war between the Native Americans and the United States government followed. The Native Americans were intent on preserving their way of life. The government was determined to open the West to exploration and settlement.

In 1866, a Sioux chief named Red Cloud declared war on the United States. The Army had built several forts along the Bozeman Trail, supposedly to guard travelers and settlers. Red Cloud and his people attacked these forts. The chief had warned government representatives, saying, "The Great Father sends us presents and wants us to sell him the road, but the White Chief comes with soldiers to steal it before we say yes or no. I will talk with you no more. I will go now and I will fight you."

Photo of Red Cloud taken in 1900

And fight he did. In one battle, all 80 men under the command of Lieutenant Colonel William Fetterman were killed. Fetterman had once boasted that he could defeat the entire Sioux Nation with a single company of 80 cavalrymen.

Although Red Cloud won the battle, many of his warriors were killed. The natives called this encounter The Battle of the Hundred Slain. The white people called it Fetterman's Massacre. It was only one of many battles during the Red Cloud War.

Present-day Sioux re-enact a battle

Chapter 4

THE CONFLICT INCREASES

For a time, Red Cloud's campaign against the whites was successful. Forts along the Bozeman Trail were abandoned.

Government officials knew something had to be done. So the Fort Laramie Treaty of 1868 was proposed. This treaty created the Great Sioux Reservation, which included the Black Hills, a sacred site for the Sioux and several other tribes. In the treaty, the federal government promised to keep white settlers out of the area. The treaty also said that the tribes could hunt in the region "as long as there were buffalo." And it said that anyone who wanted to pass through these lands had to have permission from the Sioux.

Photo of Chief American Horse and Chief Red Cloud taken in 1891

Disagreement Among the Sioux

It took federal authorities several months to convince most of the Sioux chiefs to sign the treaty. This was because the agreement contained many conditions that the Sioux refused to accept. Among other things, the government wanted them to settle in one place and become farmers.

Chief Spotted Tail was the first to sign, but he did so with objections. "There is plenty of game in our country at present," he said, "and we cannot go farming until all that is gone." Red Cloud was the last to sign.

Other chiefs refused to sign the treaty. Sitting Bull didn't even bother to attend the talks. Neither did Crazy Horse, who declared, "Now you tell us to work for a living, but the Great Spirit did not make us to work, but to live by hunting. You white men can work if you want to . . . We do not want your civilization. We would live as our fathers lived, and their fathers before them."

Photo of Chief Spotted Tail taken in 1872

The Slaughter of the Buffalo

It became apparent that a treaty alone was not going to make the Sioux change their way of life. Some Native Americans refused to move to the reservation lands. Soon the United States government decided that the Sioux would have to be forced to follow the terms of the treaty.

Once the Civil War had ended in 1865, some soldiers had become "Indian Fighters." One of these men was General William T. Sherman, who said, "Force must be used." He also wrote that it would be "a good idea to invite all the sportsmen of England and America this fall for a Great Buffalo Hunt and make a grand sweep of them all."

General Philip Sheridan agreed. He said, "For the sake of lasting peace, let them kill, skin, and sell until the buffaloes are exterminated."

Photo of General William T. Sherman taken during the Civil War

Both generals felt that the only way to make the Sioux settle on the reservation was to wipe out the buffalo. So, encouraged by the government, hunters came by the thousands.

In the early 1800s, 50 million buffalo had roamed the Great Plains. By 1870, the number was reduced to 13 million. By 1889, only 835 buffalo were left alive.

Chapter 5

GOLD IN THE HILLS

Not long after the Treaty of Fort Laramie was signed in 1868, gold was discovered in the Black Hills. The Sioux did not consider the soft yellow metal valuable. What was of value to them in the hills was a rare stone that was used to make sacred pipes. However, they quickly realized that gold "made white people crazy." Soon there was trouble between the Sioux who wanted to protect their sacred lands and the whites who wanted to search the hills for gold.

General George Custer

As commander of the 7th Cavalry Regiment, General George Custer was determined to make a name for himself. In July 1874, Custer set off on an expedition to the Black Hills. Officially, it was an exploratory survey. To support this claim, the party included a mapmaker and scientists who would study the plants, animals, and geography of the area. However, it is likely that Custer had another purpose, since he also brought two miners along. And because he always looked for publicity, he traveled with reporters and a photographer.

The Sioux talked about the expedition all that summer. Chief Red Cloud told his people that the soldiers had gone to the Black Hills to make sure other white people didn't invade the area. But most other Sioux leaders, including Sitting Bull and Crazy Horse, disagreed.

General George Custer

Photo of Custer's expedition to the Black Hills in the summer of 1874

In mid-August, newspapers across the nation were reporting that gold was plentiful in the Black Hills. By the end of that month, when Custer's expedition was officially over, hundreds of miners had rushed to the area. Soon afterward, booming towns sprang up on the sacred land of the Sioux.

The United States Army did try to contain the invasion of prospectors, but the region was too large to patrol. And the officers did not really want to punish the miners.

Black Elk's Words

In the summer of 1874, Custer's soldiers came to the Black Hills. A young man named Black Elk was eleven years old at the time. Black Elk, who would grow up to become a highly respected leader of his people, reflected on what happened.

"Afterward I learned that it was Pahuska ("Long Hair," the Sioux name for General George Custer) who had led his soldiers to see what they could find," said Black Elk. "He had no right to go in there, because all that country was ours. Also the wasichus (white men) had made a treaty with Red Cloud that said it would be ours as long as grass should grow and water flow. Later I learned, too, that Pahuska had found there much of the yellow metal that makes the wasichus crazy; and that is what made the bad trouble, just as it did before . . ."

Black Elk added, "Our people knew there was yellow metal in little chunks up there; but they did not bother with it, because it was not good for anything."

Chapter 6

SELLING THE LAND

By September 1875, the federal government was talking about leasing or buying the land in the Black Hills. A group of white men met with the Sioux to discuss the matter. At first, the Sioux leaders didn't understand the meaning of the word lease. When they realized it was a form of selling the land, they were outraged.

At one point during the meetings, 300 warriors arrived. Little Big Man, their leader, said, "Black Hills is my land and I love it, and whoever interferes will hear this gun." Then he threatened, "I will kill the first chief who speaks for selling the Black Hills." In addition, his close friend, Crazy Horse, had given him a message to deliver: "One does not sell the land the people walk on."

Sitting Bull, Crazy Horse, and their followers were determined to defend the land. However, some Native Americans felt differently. Many were starving and sick.

Chiefs like Red Cloud and Spotted Tail realized that their world was changing. They knew their people needed help. They thought that by selling the Black Hills to the government, they would receive this help.

Setting a Price

Red Cloud wanted to be sure his people got enough money to make giving up their land worthwhile. He said, "I think that the Black Hills are worth more than all the wild beasts and all the tame beasts in the possession of the white people . . . but now you want to take them away from me and make me poor, so I ask so much that I won't be poor."

He requested 70 million dollars. He wanted to be sure that his people had food, clothing, and shelter forever.

Photo of Little Big Man taken in 1876

Government representatives came back with two different offers. They would pay $400,000 a year to lease the land. Or they would buy the land for 6 million dollars, given to the Sioux in 15 separate payments.

The Sioux turned down both offers and the talks ended.

Sitting Bull's Vision

In 1876, the United States marked its centennial—the 100th anniversary of the nation's independence. While the rest of the country planned celebrations, the army prepared to launch a campaign against the "hostile" tribes who lived off the reservations. Troops first attacked several Cheyenne villages, mistaking them for camps belonging to Sitting Bull and Crazy Horse.

In early June, the Sioux who lived in the Rosebud River area of southeastern Montana held their annual Sun Dance. During the dance, Sitting Bull had a vision. He saw white men falling into his camp. In his vision, the men were dead. Sitting Bull said the men had no ears because white men "never listen."

Portrait of Sitting Bull painted in 1890

A few weeks later, Crazy Horse and General George Crook met in battle near the Rosebud River. Crook, who had gained fame as an Indian fighter in Oklahoma, was new to the area. Although he won the battle, his troops were left in bad shape and retreated to their base camp.

Sitting Bull didn't believe that this was the event he had seen in his vision. He and his people moved a short distance west to a valley near the Little Big Horn River, where they were joined by members of the Cheyenne and Arapaho tribes. There were reports of antelope and other game animals in the area so the hunting would be good. And there would be plenty of grass for the horses to eat.

Custer's Last Battle

On June 25, 1876, General Custer and his 7th Army Cavalry advanced from the north toward Sitting Bull's camp. Custer had more than 200 men. Major Marcus Reno and another 112 men came from the south.

Major Reno and his men arrived at the camp first. From the start, things didn't go as expected. Custer had predicted that the natives would flee, but they didn't. Also, the support the general had promised Reno didn't arrive. After only 45 minutes of fighting, the major turned back. About half of his men had been killed in the brief battle.

Meanwhile, Custer and his troops approached along the bluffs that ran beside the east bank of the Little Big Horn River.

No one knows what Custer thought when he discovered the camp was larger than he had expected. Many of his scouts ran off in panic at the sight of so many warriors. Before leaving, they warned Custer that the situation looked hopeless. What is known is that Custer sent a message asking for help from other troops in the area. In it, he said, "Come on. Big village. Be quick. Bring packs. Hurry."

In about 25 minutes, the battle was over. Crazy Horse led his men forward, yelling, “It is a good day to fight! It is a good day to die! Strong hearts, brave hearts, to the front! Weak hearts and cowards to the rear!”

Sioux at a re-enactment of Custer’s Last Stand

There was only one survivor from the 7th Cavalry—a horse. When the other troops arrived, it was too late. They found Custer's body near the body of a New York City journalist. The man had been brought to report on the general's success in battle.

The news reached the rest of the country in July. The event was treated as a national tragedy. Poets wrote poems about "Custer's Last Stand" and the "Custer Massacre." The people of the United States demanded revenge.

The reporting was totally one-sided. Few people cared about the concerns of the Native Americans.

This painting of Custer's Last Stand was created in 1889.

THE GHOST DANCE AND ITS AFTERMATH

The Sioux and their allies fought desperately to preserve their way of life. However, winning the Battle of Little Big Horn actually signaled the end of that life. As punishment for the massacre, the federal government took away much of the land that had been part of the Great Sioux Reservation. By 1889, there were just six small reservations in its place.

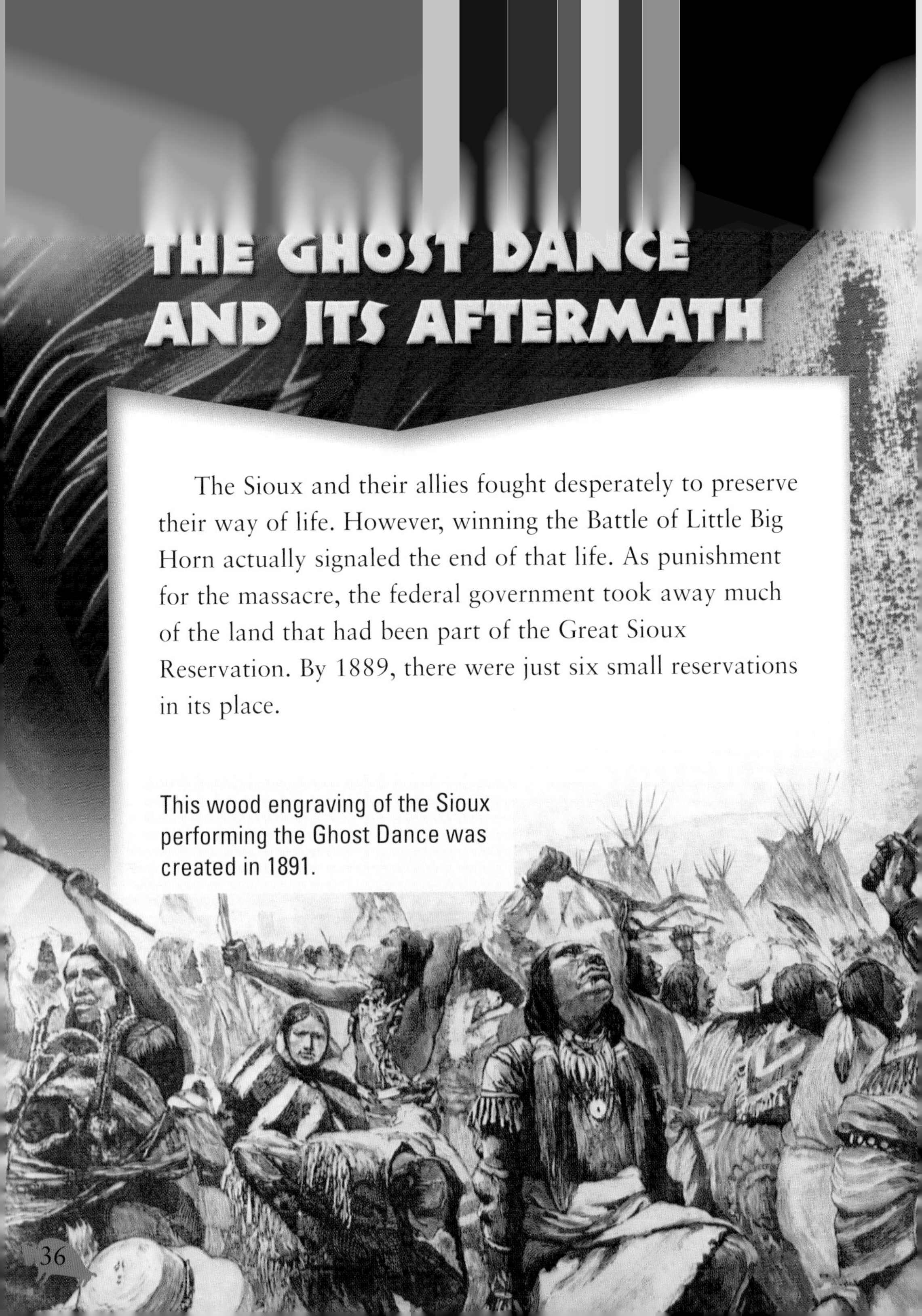

This wood engraving of the Sioux performing the Ghost Dance was created in 1891.

A Prophecy

Sometime in 1889, in Nebraska, a Paiute holy man named Wovoka had a vision. In his vision, he saw a way to make the white men go away. Afterward, he made a prophecy. He told his people that by practicing his teachings and dancing a sacred "Ghost Dance," their land would be returned to them. The buffalo and other wild creatures would come back. There would be peace and good fortune for the natives of the Great Plains.

News of this prophecy quickly reached other tribes. The Ghost Dance became very popular. In the summer of 1890, the Sioux adopted the dance. They changed it somewhat, adding touches of their own to the ceremony. A special shirt was created for the dance. It was supposed to protect the dancers from the white soldiers' bullets.

Every time another Ghost Dance began, the federal agents on the reservations became frightened and sent tribal police to put a stop to the ceremony.

The Battle of Wounded Knee

The Ghost Dances made the settlers and soldiers fear more attacks from the natives. On the evening of December 28, 1890, the cavalry attacked a camp at Wounded Knee Creek. By the next afternoon, nearly 300 Sioux had been killed. Most of them were unarmed and helpless. Two-thirds of those killed were women and children. After a two-day blizzard, the frozen bodies were recovered and given a mass burial.

Black Elk saw the site not long after the battle. Later he would say, "I did not know then how much was ended. When I look back now from this high hill of my old age, I can still see the women and children lying heaped and scattered all along the crooked gulch as plain as when I saw them with eyes still young. And I can see that something else died there in the bloody mud, and was buried in the blizzard. A people's dream died there. It was a beautiful dream."

This 1891 illustration shows the Battle of Wounded Knee.

Ninety Years Later

Not everyone approved of what had happened to the Native Americans. However, it was many years before anything was officially done about the matter. In 1980, the United States Supreme Court issued a statement. It said, "A more ripe and rank case of dishonorable dealing will never, in all probability, be found in our history."

The Indian Claims Bureau then awarded the Sioux Nation 100 million dollars in compensation for taking the Black Hills. The tribe refused to take the money, saying that the Black Hills were not for sale at any price.

The money still remains in the national treasury, earning interest. Representatives of the Sioux Nation say that all they want is their sacred land back. The claims continue to this day.

Index